Becoming the Man, You're Meant to Be:

10 Techniques for Discovering Authentic Masculinity

By

Calvin L. Willis

ISBN: 979-8-89397-789-9

Edition: First

Published by Booklyn Writers

Heartfelt Author's Note

Dear Reader,

This guide is born from my personal journey through challenges, failures, and ultimate triumph. As someone who has faced darkness and discovered light, my deepest desire is to help you uncover your true potential. You are not alone on this path, and my hope is that this guide serves as a trusted companion as you navigate your way to becoming an authentic man.

The techniques, tools, and stories shared here are inspired by wisdom that has transformed lives — from the profound teachings of Dr. Myles Munroe to the timeless principles of Stoicism. Together, these lessons are meant to guide you toward strength, resilience, and purpose.

Let this journey be one of self-discovery, growth, and empowerment. Remember, becoming the man you're meant to be is not about perfection but about embracing your authentic self.

With sincerity,

Calvin L. Willis

Table of Contents

Introduction

Authentic masculinity is not about dominance or bravado; it's about integrity, purpose, and resilience. In this guide, we'll explore ten techniques to help you discover your true self and embrace the man you're meant to be. These techniques are practical, reflective, and rooted in wisdom from both modern and ancient teachings.

About the Author

Authur Calvin L. Willis is a man who has walked through the fire and emerged with a purpose. His journey—from a childhood marked by mental, emotional, physical, and sexual abuse to years spent in group homes, foster care, juvenile detention, and adult incarceration—has shaped him into a mentor, guide, and leader. After overcoming 22 years in prison and years of drug addiction, Calvin dedicated himself to self-transformation, determined to understand his purpose and align with God's plan for his life. Like Moses, who endured trials before realizing his divine calling, Calvin's struggles became the foundation for his mission: to help others navigate life's toughest obstacles. Through his writing, speaking, and nonprofit work, he equips young people with the tools they need to become leaders. His books seamlessly blend Stoic philosophy, timeless wisdom, and real-life lessons, offering practical guidance for mastering emotions, relationships, and personal growth. Driven by resilience and faith, Calvin L. Willis is more than an author—he is a testament to the power of redemption, purpose, and perseverance.

Chapter 1

Embrace Responsibility

Guide: Responsibility is the foundation of authentic manhood. Start small by owning your actions, decisions, and their consequences.

Tool: Create a responsibility journal. Every night, write one thing you took responsibility for during the day. Reflect on how it made you feel.

True Story:

James, a 14-year-old, struggled with anger after his parents' divorce. Taking responsibility for his emotions, he started journaling his thoughts. Over time, he learned to communicate his feelings rather than acting out. This simple step transformed his relationships.

Chapter 2

Master Your Emotions

Guide: Emotional mastery is not suppression but understanding and channeling your feelings constructively.

Tool: Practice the "pause" technique. When angry or upset, take a deep breath, count to ten, and re-evaluate your reaction.

True Story:

Andre, 16, used to lash out when criticized. Inspired by Marcus Aurelius, he began practicing the pause technique. This allowed him to respond thoughtfully instead of reacting impulsively, earning him respect from peers and teachers alike.

Chapter 3

Develop Discipline

Guide: Discipline is the bridge between goals and accomplishments. Start by creating daily routines that align with your aspirations.

Tool: Use the "1-1-1 Rule" — set one goal, complete one task, and celebrate one win every day.

True Story:

Michael, 17, wanted to improve his grades but felt overwhelmed. By focusing on one small goal daily, he gradually built the discipline to study consistently, leading to academic success.

Chapter 4

Seek Wisdom

Guide: Authentic men are lifelong learners. Seek wisdom from books, mentors, and experiences.

Tool: Read one book monthly on personal growth. Begin with The Principles and Power of Vision by Dr. Myles Munroe and Meditations by Marcus Aurelius.

True Story:

Ethan, 15, found himself lost in peer pressure. Reading Dr. Munroe's book inspired him to envision a future beyond temporary distractions, leading him to pursue his passion for photography.

Chapter 5

Cultivate Courage

Guide: Courage is not the absence of fear but the willingness to act despite it.

Tool: Write down one fear holding you back. Take a small, intentional step toward facing it this week.

True Story:

Jason, 13, was terrified of public speaking. By starting with small presentations in front of his family, he gained confidence and eventually delivered a powerful speech at school.

Chapter 6
Build Meaningful Relationships

Guide: Surround yourself with people who uplift and challenge you.

Tool: Identify three people who inspire you and schedule time to learn from them.

True Story:

Luis, 14, joined a mentorship program and found guidance from a coach who encouraged him to excel in academics and sports. This relationship became a turning point in his life.

Chapter 7

Find Your Purpose

Guide: Purpose gives direction to your life. Reflect on what brings you joy and where you can make a difference.

Tool: Write your "life purpose statement" by answering these questions: What am I good at? What do I love? How can I serve others?

True Story:

Derrick, 16, discovered his passion for coding by asking these questions. Today, he's developing apps that help his community.

Chapter 8

Practice Gratitude

Guide: Gratitude shifts your focus from what you lack to what you have.

Tool: Keep a gratitude jar. Write one thing you're thankful for every day and place it in the jar.

True Story:

Antonio, 15, struggled with feelings of inadequacy. Practicing gratitude helped him recognize his blessings and approach life with positivity.

Chapter 9
Maintain Integrity

Guide: Integrity is doing what's right even when no one is watching.

Tool: Use the "mirror test." Before making a decision, ask yourself if you'll be proud to face yourself in the mirror afterward.

True Story:

Mark, 17, was tempted to cheat during an exam but chose honesty. His decision earned him trust and respect, proving that integrity is always rewarding.

Chapter 10

Serve Others

Guide: True masculinity is about lifting others.

Tool: Volunteer for a cause you care about. Serving others will bring fulfillment and perspective.

True Story:

Samuel, 16, began helping at a local shelter. The experience not only made a difference in others' lives but also gave him a sense of purpose.

Heartfelt Conclusion

Becoming an authentic man is a journey, not a destination. Each step you take, every lesson you learn, and every challenge you overcome shapes the person you are meant to be. Remember, you are not alone in this journey. Take these teachings, tools, and stories to heart, and let them guide you toward a life of integrity, purpose, and fulfillment.

With unwavering belief in your potential,

Calvin L. Willis